GHOST DETECTORS

Honk!

BOOK 8

BY
DOTTI ENDERLE

ILLUSTRATED BY
HOWARD MCWILLIAM

magic
wagon

visit us at www.abdopublishing.com

A big thank you to Adrienne Enderle — DE
With thanks to my ever supportive wife Rebecca — HM

Printed in the United States of America, Melrose Park, Illinois.
042011
092011

 This book contains at least 10% recycled materials.

Text by Dotti Enderle
Illustrations by Howard McWilliam
Edited by Stephanie Hedlund and Rochelle Baltzer
Cover and interior design by Jaime Martens

Library of Congress Cataloging-in-Publication Data

Enderle, Dotti, 1954-
  Honk! / by Dotti Enderle ; illustrated by Howard McWilliam.
     p. cm. -- (Ghost Detectors ; bk. 8)
  ISBN 978-1-61641-624-9
  [1. School buses--Fiction. 2. Ghosts--Fiction. 3. Humorous stories.]
I. McWilliam, Howard, 1977- ill. II. Title.
  PZ7.E69645Ho 2011
  [Fic]--dc22
                              2011001840

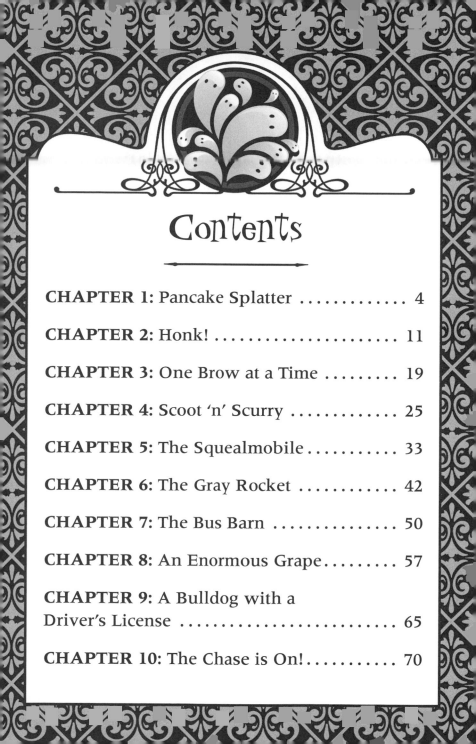

Contents

Pancake Splatter

Malcolm was well aware that he had one eye open and one eye closed. But it was six o'clock in the morning. Everyone was half asleep at that hour. He was sure the other eye would wake up by seven. Actually, it happened sooner.

"Ahhhhhhh!" his sister, Cocoa, screamed into the kitchen.

His mom happened to be flipping a pancake at that moment. She jerked the spatula, causing the pancake to somersault

up and away from the griddle and land on one of Cocoa's bejeweled sneakers.

"Ahhhhh!" Cocoa screamed even louder.

Malcolm's other eye popped open, but now the hearing in one of his ears was shattered.

Grandma Eunice, whose wheelchair was stuck between the kitchen door and the hallway, clacked her dentures. "Hey! That was my pancake!"

"Who cares about your old pancake?" Cocoa whined.

Grandma shoved the wheelchair in, chipping a piece of wood off the doorjamb. "I care," she said. "I'm on one of those whole grain diets, and that was a wheat pancake."

Malcolm grinned. "Now it's shoe polish," he said, pointing to Cocoa's sneaker.

Cocoa kicked her foot. The pancake flew across the room and stuck to the wall just above the toaster oven.

Malcolm was glad that both eyes were open for that trick, but he noticed that his father stayed hidden behind his newspaper. Dad had mastered the art of staying out of drama.

"What's the problem, Cocoa?" Mom asked.

Cocoa stood there in her pink-and-red striped T-shirt and puke-green pants. Her shoes looked like someone had glued plastic rhinestones to mildewed gym sneakers. Well, one of the sneakers looked like that. The other now had the added pizzazz of whole wheat pancake batter.

"I'll tell you the problem," she said. "This!" She pushed back her frizzy bangs. Part of her left eyebrow was missing.

Malcolm fell off his chair laughing.

"Oh dear!" Mom exclaimed.

Dad glanced over his newspaper, then went back to reading.

Grandma Eunice rolled up for a better look. "I guess that makes us even," she said. "You have half an eyebrow. I have half a pancake."

"What happened?" Mom asked.

"I was waxing my eyebrows when a bunch of the hot wax spilled across my forehead. I tried to wipe it off with a rag, but the rag stuck. It ripped off part of my brow!"

"It'll grow back," Mom said.

Cocoa stomped her pancake-battered foot. "That could take weeks! I can't go out looking like this. I'm hideous!"

"Actually, I think it's an improvement," Malcolm said.

Cocoa batted the back of his head with her hand.

"Ouch! Mom, she hit me!"

Mom did her usual eye roll. "Cut it out, both of you."

"What will become of me?" Cocoa cried. "I'll be forced to stay in. I'll have to be homeschooled. No more dances, pep rallies, or voice lessons."

"Actually," Malcolm interjected, "that last one is a good thing."

He ducked before the next swat landed on the back of his head.

Mom put her arm around Cocoa's shoulders and stroked her bushy hair. "You won't become a shut-in," she assured

her. "I have an eyebrow pencil that will fix that right up."

Cocoa whimpered, then she followed Mom down the hall. Malcolm turned back in time to see Grandma Eunice scrape the pancake of the wall.

She wheeled around and clacked her dentures. "Now, where's the syrup?"

Honk!

Waiting for the school day to end was like waiting for a snail to cross a football field. Malcolm continually watched the clock. When the bell finally rang, he was on his feet and ready to go.

What a day! Mrs. Goolsby had turned the fifth-grade class into a torture chamber. He'd suffered through a major science test, two pop quizzes, and an hour-long lecture on Andrew Jackson—whose parrot had to be removed from Jackson's funeral for

swearing too much. Actually, Malcolm liked that part. The thought of a cussing parrot was hilarious.

Now, Malcolm and Dandy hurried out the double doors and stood in line. They were waiting to get on the bus. But where was it?

"How come our bus isn't here?" Dandy asked as he held his backpack, lunch box, and jacket in his arms. It looked like the contents of a storage closet had been dumped on top of him.

Malcolm strained to look down the road. "I don't know. Maybe it broke down again."

The other bus riders had questioning looks as well. "Your temporary bus will be here momentarily," one teacher informed the group. "Bus 277 broke down again."

Malcolm wasn't surprised. Bus 277 didn't run like other buses. It galloped instead. Malcolm had finally gotten used to his backside taking a pounding. But no matter how tightly Dandy held on, he still managed to bump his head on the ceiling at least three times riding to and from school.

"No more Bus 277?" Dandy asked, smiling and rubbing his head.

Malcolm smiled too. "Not for a while, I guess."

It was another five minutes or so before their replacement bus, number 445, drove into the circle drive. Mr. Mullins, their regular bus driver, was hunched behind the wheel. *Honk!*

"He doesn't have to honk," Dandy said. "We can see he's here."

Honk!

The bus door cranked open and Mr. Mullins shrugged. "Sorry about the horn. Don't know why it keeps honking. It must be out of whack. It honks on its own."

Malcolm was okay with that. An occasional honk wasn't nearly as bad as the rickety ride he usually suffered. Riding the old bus was like going to school in a tumble dryer. Besides, he was used to noise. This loud honking didn't compare to the ear-splitting shrieks of his sister.

The students loaded in, scuffling down the aisle to the back. Dandy dropped his backpack, lunch box, and jacket on the gunky floor. He rested his feet on top of the pile. His knees were practically up to his chin.

"How long do you think we'll be riding this bus?" he asked.

Malcolm lowered the window. "I hope for a long time."

"I hope forever," Dandy said.

"Dandy, we won't be going to school forever. And we definitely won't be going to Waxberry Elementary forever."

Dandy scratched a knee, which was incredibly close to his nose. "Do you think school buses will change by the time we go to high school?"

"Change how?" Malcolm asked.

Dandy scratched the other knee. "It's a long time before we go to high school. Maybe school buses will be more advanced. You know, futuristic."

"You mean equipped with extra gadgets like a DVD player, video games, and a soda dispenser?"

Dandy scratched his knee with his chin. "No, I mean maybe they'll fly."

Malcolm shook his head. "Buses won't fly when we're in high school."

"That'd be cool though, huh?" Dandy said.

Malcolm couldn't deny it. "That would be cool."

Honk!

The horn beeped so loudly that Malcolm nearly flew out of his seat. Dandy flinched, bumping his nose on his knee. He rubbed it, then checked for blood.

"I can't believe the horn just honks by itself," Malcolm said. He peeked up the aisle at Mr. Mullins.

Honk!

Mr. Mullins looked back at them through his oversized rearview mirror. "Just try to ignore it," he said loudly. "I'll make sure it's fixed before tomorrow morning."

The drivers passing by were glaring in anger. One stuck out his tongue.

Honk!

Malcolm sat back. "Those people think Mr. Mullins is honking at them. They're pretty mad."

"Yeah," Dandy agreed. "But they're also getting out of the way in a hurry. We'll get home pretty quick at this rate."

Honk!

Malcolm nodded. "Maybe a stuck horn is a good thing."

"You know what would be even better?" Dandy said, scratching his chin with his knee. "If the bus could fly."

Honk!

One Brow at a Time

The bus gave one more good *honk* as Malcolm stepped off. Mr. Mullins stepped on the gas and Bus 445 chugged away.

It felt good to finally be home. After grabbing an apple from the kitchen, Malcolm hurried toward his room. But when he walked by the bathroom he did a double take.

Cocoa was perched on the counter, holding up a magnifying mirror that made

her eye appear about the size of a melon. If this were a science fiction movie, she'd be the attacking alien. If only he had a laser to take her down.

There was a tube of glue by the sink. A pair of tweezers was in Cocoa's hand, and a woolly, brown sweater was in her lap.

Malcolm just couldn't turn away. "I'm almost afraid to ask, but what are you doing?" he finally said.

"Like it's any of your business," she spat.

She plucked a piece of fuzz from the sweater and carefully held it with the tweezers like it might be the last piece of lint in existence. She dipped a delicate end to the glue then daintily attached it to her bald brow.

"Really?" Malcolm said. "You're going to glue a thousand of those fibers to your face?"

"Shut up, nerd!" She plucked another.

"Your real eyebrows will grow back by the time you get all those on."

"I'm not just using the sweater, pea-brain. I plucked some hairs from my other eyebrow so it'll look more natural."

Malcolm laughed. "But it's not natural. The glue shows. It's not the same color as your skin."

"Like I haven't figured that out," she smirked. "I plan to wear glue-color eye shadow to match."

"Yeah . . . that'll work."

"Get out of here!" Using her foot, Cocoa slammed the door shut.

Malcolm was nearly to his room when his mom hurried into the hall. She had her purse in one hand and car keys in the other.

"Hey, I need you to come with us," she said.

"Where?" he asked.

Mom fiddled with the keys. "I'm taking Grandma Eunice to Scoot 'n' Scurry."

"Scoot 'n' Scurry?" Malcolm repeated.

She jingled the keys, an indication that she was in a rush. "It's a store that sells scooters for senior citizens."

Malcolm suddenly had a vision of Grandma Eunice sailing down the sidewalk on a scooter, one foot on, the other pushing it along.

"Grandma can barely stand up," he reminded her. "How can she propel a scooter?"

"It's an electric scooter, silly. Sort of like the ones you see in the grocery store, only smaller. Now let's go," she pressed.

"Why do I have to go?"

Mom thumped her foot impatiently. "Because I need someone to help me with Grandma."

"Why can't Cocoa do it?"

Mom looked toward the bathroom and sighed. "I could barely get her to go to school this morning. I don't think she'll be leaving the house very much for a while."

After a rough day at school and the blaring horn on the way home, Malcolm was ready to relax. He wanted to play video games, watch TV, or have a game of fetch with his ghostly dog, Spooky. He simply didn't want to leave.

He was about to protest again when an ear-popping screech came from the bathroom. Malcolm knew he was defeated.

"Darn it! I can't get these lashes to stick!" Cocoa yelled.

"Quick, let's go," Malcolm said as they scurried to the front door.

Scoot 'n' Scurry

Scoot 'n' Scurry looked like a mini car dealership. Several scooters were showcased in the large, polished windows. They came in all shapes and sizes.

They'd barely made it through the door when a man with slick black hair and horn-rimmed glasses approached.

"Hello," he said. "Welcome to Scoot 'n' Scurry. My name is Lawrence Linkletter,

but you may call me LL. Can I help you find something?"

Malcolm checked out the name tag attached to the man's pocket. It read: LL, Senior Sales Associate.

"Do you sell scooters here?" Grandma asked.

LL looked around at the dozens of scooters in the showroom. "Uh, yes."

"Good. Cause my wheelchair is big and bulky and scraping the walls. I need something new. Something motorized. Something space age. But I have to warn you, I don't have a license."

"Not to worry," LL said. "You don't need a license to drive one of these."

Malcolm laughed. "You don't know my grandma. She just might."

"Hush, Malcolm," Mom said. She guided Grandma Eunice over to a red and black model with four small wheels. "Here. Let's try this one."

LL's eyes lit up. "Good choice."

Grandma dropped down onto the squishy seat. She gripped the handle, then looked down. "Where's the gas pedal?"

"It's electric," LL said. He handed her the remote.

Grandma Eunice pressed the Go button. The scooter pushed forward with the speed of a pencil rolling uphill. After traveling a few feet, she turned it around and stopped. "Attach a blade and I could mow the lawn with this thing."

LL put on a fake grin. "Let's try another."

Mom pointed to a sleek green three-wheeler with a cushy white seat and white handlebar. "Maybe this one."

"Yes," said LL. "Maximum control."

Malcolm helped Grandma Eunice on.

LL leaned forward. "This one is quite easy," he assured her. "Just twist the handgrip this way to go forward, and this way to back up."

He barely finished speaking when Grandma took off, nearly running over Malcolm's foot. She did some twists and turns and a couple of donuts.

"How does that feel?" LL asked.

Grandma's mouth twitched. "Do you have something with two wheels?"

LL was starting to sweat a little. "No, ma'am. You'll have to visit a Harley dealership for that."

"That one looks space age," Grandma said, pointing to a bucket seat with wheels.

Malcolm had to admit it did look space age. Like something from the Starship Enterprise. Grandma Eunice could really blast off in that.

"And you'd look wonderful powering it," LL said in a squirmy salesman voice.

Then Grandma saw the price tag. "Wow!" she exclaimed. "For this price, it better travel to the moon!"

LL bit at one of his nails. "Maybe you'd like to see our closeout models?"

"Yes," Mom said. "That would be better."

LL led them to an orange and purple scooter that looked like a skateboard with a seat. There were signs plastered all

around it shouting *BARGAIN!!! BARGAIN!!! BARGAIN!!!*

Grandma clapped her hands. "Three exclamation marks! This must be a winner."

Malcolm looked around for the other closeouts. So did Mom.

"This is it?" Mom asked.

LL bit another nail. "I'm afraid so. But you can't go wrong with this baby."

Malcolm somehow doubted it.

Grandma wasted no time climbing on. "This is a beaut." She pressed the remote and the scooter quietly sped forward. She zoomed around the store, banging against boxes, knocking over display signs, and scraping LL's desk.

"This one's perfect!" she announced as she careened back.

"Don't you think it's just a little too fast?" Mom asked.

Grandma waved the question away. "Honey, after a breakfast of whole wheat and prunes, I need something fast."

Mom gulped and looked at LL. "We'll take it."

LL beamed. "Great! Now, can I interest you in a ramp?"

"No thanks," Mom said. "We already have one."

Oh yeah, Malcolm thought. *He meant a wheelchair ramp.*

"By the way," LL said. He steepled his fingers together and knitted his brow. "This is a closeout item. No returns. No refunds."

Grandma Eunice chirped, "I won't need a refund. It's perfect."

She insisted on driving her new scooter over to the car. "Look. It has a horn." *Beep! Beep! Beep!*

Malcolm put his hands over his ears. Uh-oh. Not a horn!

The Squealmobile

*H*onk!

"Guess they didn't get it fixed," Dandy said as he and Malcolm climbed on to Bus 445.

Mr. Mullins gave them a grouchy frown. The constant honking was driving him batty. He jerked the lever to close the door.

Honk! Honk!

"No," he barked. "It's not fixed."

All the students were cowering in their seats. Malcolm was thankful that he and Dandy always sat in the back.

Honk!

"It's going to be a long ride to school," Malcolm whispered.

The bus trundled along, honking at each stop. Mr. Mullins gritted his teeth and gripped the wheel with white knuckles.

Hooooooonk!

He hit at the wheel with this fist. "Stop it!" he yelled.

Hooooooonk!

Mr. Mullins looked like he was one fist-pound away from a full tantrum.

"Something's wrong," Malcolm said just as the horn blared again.

"What'd you say?" Dandy asked.

"I said, something is wrong."

Dandy cupped his hands behind his ears. "Huh?"

Hooooooonk!

"This whole thing just doesn't feel right to me."

Hooooooonk!

Dandy leaned closer. "What?"

Hooooooonk!

Malcolm gave up and sat back. "Never mind."

His ears were ringing by the time they got to school.

Everyone was on their feet, ready to exit as fast as they could. Mr. Mullins pulled the lever to open the door. Nothing happened. He pulled harder.

"What's going on?" Mr. Mullins mumbled.

Hooooooonk!

He grabbed the lever with both hands and pulled. Nothing. "The door's jammed."

Malcolm tilted his head toward Dandy. "What are the odds that both the horn and the door are broken?"

Dandy fidgeted a little. "Pretty good, I'd say. Looks like we're trapped."

"We're not trapped," Malcolm assured him. A third-grade girl climbed over the seats, hurdling toward the front.

Mr. Mullins now had his foot on the dashboard for leverage as he tugged.

Malcolm pushed past a couple of students behind him and popped open the emergency doors. "We're not trapped."

Those were his last words before a flood of panicked students plowed over him to get off.

As soon as they were out and on the sidewalk, the side door slid open. Mr. Mullins looked like he just lost a wrestling match. His beet-red face was soaked with sweat, and he huffed and puffed for breath.

"I'll get it fixed by this afternoon," he wheezed.

Hooooooonk!

Mrs. Goolsby went much easier on them today. No tests. No pop quizzes. No oral reports. Maybe she felt bad about their agony of riding to school in "the Squealmobile" as everyone was now calling it. Some students were still shaking at lunch.

For the first time in his life, Malcolm dreaded the last bell. He and Dandy dragged along, making their way to the double doors.

"He got it fixed, right?" Dandy asked, lugging his overloaded backpack.

"I'm sure he got it fixed," Malcolm said. Though he was not so sure. "If it's not fixed, then he'll drive us home in a different bus."

Dandy heaved the backpack along, walking slower and slower. "I never thought I'd miss old 277. Bumping my head wasn't so bad."

As they reached the double doors they could see the drooping faces of the other bus riders. You'd think they were all called to the principal's office. Although sitting in the principal's office was nothing compared to sitting on Bus 445.

When the door cranked open, Mr. Mullins stood with both hands up in a "stop right there" motion.

"It's okay," he began. "We replaced several parts. It passed inspection. And it didn't honk once on the way here. We also oiled up the door and lever. It's just like new."

Malcolm sighed and nudged Dandy. "I told you it'd be fixed."

The ride home went smoothly until the stop before Malcolm's. Mr. Mullins pulled over and turned on the red flashing lights. A few students filed out. But then Audrey Miller, a second grader, stepped over to exit.

Before she could step down, she tripped on absolutely nothing. She bounced down the steps on her bottom and landed on the grass.

"Oh no!" Mr. Mullins called, rushing down to help her.

Malcolm, Dandy, and the remaining passengers hopped up to see what was going on.

"Did you see that?" Malcolm blurted out, not believing his eyes.

"Yeah," Dandy said. "Her feet came right out from under her! You think someone dropped a banana peel?"

Malcolm shook his head. "I didn't see a banana peel."

Dandy leaned over the seat, trying to get a better look. "Maybe she slipped on some of that oil they used to fix the door."

Malcolm didn't see any oily spots. "Or maybe she was dragged out the door," he suggested.

"That's just silly, Malcolm. Nobody was around," Dandy replied.

Malcolm cocked an eyebrow. "Because the thing that pulled her didn't have a body."

Dandy scratched his head. "Huh?"

"Dandy, Bus 445 has a ghost."

Hooooooonk!

The Gray Rocket

Dandy called home to tell his mom that he'd be at Malcolm's for a while. Then just as they were headed to the basement lab—*Beep! Beep!*

Grandma Eunice swerved around the corner on her new scooter. She had on a leather jacket, Cocoa's old bicycle helmet, and swim goggles.

"Look out!" she warned. "Biker Granny is on the loose!"

She whipped the scooter around again, bumping into a small table and toppling a vase. After backing up, she circled around and came to a stop just inches from Dandy's toes.

"What'd you think, Alfred?" she asked Dandy as she lifted the goggles up onto her forehead.

"Nice," Dandy said. "I especially like the decals."

"Yeah, I added those today," she bragged.

Malcolm checked it out. Grandma Eunice had applied five stickers in various places on the scooter. He read them.

Mean Machine

Fear This!

The Gray Rocket

Been There, Broke That

Danger Ranger

"You forgot one," Malcolm said. "I brake for nothing."

Grandma Eunice laughed as she lowered her goggles. She revved her scooter, bumped into the wall, and knocked down a family portrait.

Dandy's mouth hung open a little. "Why'd your grandma get a scooter?"

Malcolm opened the basement door. "Because her wheelchair was doing too much damage."

It was deadly quiet in Malcolm's basement lab. Too quiet. He relaxed on the beanbag while Dandy sat on the floor.

Dandy looked around. "Where's your dog?"

Malcolm powered up his Ecto-Handheld-Automatic-Heat-Sensitive-Laser-Enhanced Specter Detector.

Yip! Yip!

Dandy whistled. "Here, Spooky! Come on, boy."

The phantom dog jumped toward Dandy, passing right through his hands.

Malcolm was concentrating on something far more important. "It has to be a ghost."

Dandy grabbed a tennis ball. "Fetch!" he said, rolling it into a corner.

Yip! Yip! Spooky chased after the ball.

"Are you sure?" Dandy asked. "Maybe Audrey just slipped. It happens you know."

"You saw it, Dandy. Did it look like she simply slipped? Especially on a bus with a self-honking horn and jammed doors. A bus with the numbers 445."

"Yeah, that's definitely strange. But what's so weird about the numbers 445?"

"Do the math," Malcolm said. "445. $4 + 4 + 5 = 13$."

Dandy cringed. "We're riding Bus 13?"

Malcolm slowly nodded.

Spooky crouched in the corner, working furiously to bite down on the tennis ball. *Yip! Yip!*

"One day he's actually going to pick that ball up and bring it back," Dandy teased.

Malcolm looked at the specter detector he held in his hand. "We've got to get on that bus and find out who's haunting it."

Dandy's eyes lit up. "You want to take the specter detector on the bus? What if you get caught? Or worse, what if the ghost appears right there in front of everyone! I wouldn't want Mr. Mullins to freak out while he's driving us to school."

"Don't be silly. I'm not going to power it up on the way to school. That'd be crazy," Malcolm said.

Dandy retrieved the ball from the corner and bounced it on the floor. "Well, you'd have to do it going to or from school. That's the only time we're on the bus."

Yip! Yip! Spooky bounced along with the ball.

"There is another way," Malcolm said.

Dandy missed catching the ball and it dribbled back to the corner. "Malcolm, you're not thinking of doing something dumb, are you?"

"It depends on what you consider dumb."

Dandy looked a bit panicked. "Something that will get us into trouble."

"Relax. We'll only get in trouble if we get caught."

Dandy gulped. "That's what I'm afraid of."

Malcolm turned off the specter detector and Spooky vanished with a final *yip!*

"You know where the bus barn is?" he asked Dandy.

"No," Dandy answered, shaking his head.

Malcolm grinned. "Well, I do."

The Bus Barn

Dandy ran home to grab his bike. Then he and Malcolm pedaled at great speed to get to their destination.

A few shortcuts were necessary. They zoomed through Mrs. Dilly's patio, cut through the alley behind the Mini-Mart, and jumped the curb at the Maple Street red light. They were on a serious mission. One that had to be completed before dark.

Just three short blocks from the high school sat the bus barn. But it was more

than just a barn. There were rows and rows of buses lined up like yellow teeth.

Dandy pressed his face against the chain-link fence that surrounded the lot. His nose poked through one fence hole, and his mouth through another. "How are we going to find it?"

Malcolm gripped the fence and shook it. "First we have to figure a way to get inside."

They crept around, keeping an eye out for a straggling bus driver or security guard.

"Looks like everyone's gone home," Malcolm said. "Now's our chance."

Dandy smushed his face against the fence again. "But the gate's padlocked."

"We're not going through the gate." Malcolm clutched the heavy mesh of the

fence and pulled himself up. His backpack weighed him down a bit, but not enough to hold him back.

Dandy pulled his face away and looked up. "It's really tall, Malcolm. I'm afraid of heights."

"It's not so bad," Malcolm called down.

"I bet it's twenty feet high!" Dandy said with a squeak in his voice.

"I think it's only about half that, Dandy."

Dandy still stood firmly on the ground. "Maybe I could squeeze through the gate."

Malcolm paused and peered down. "A ferret couldn't squeeze through that gate. Just close your eyes and climb."

Dandy shaded his eyes with his hand. "How will I know I'm at the top if I have my eyes closed?"

"Because I'll tell you," Malcolm assured him.

Dandy took a deep breath, closed his eyes, and felt his way to the top—link by link by link.

"You can open your eyes now," Malcolm said.

Dandy slowly lifted his lids, then swayed a little from dizziness. "Yikes! How are we going to get down?"

"Like this!" Malcolm climbed over the top, turned himself around, and leaped off the fence and onto a school bus just a foot or so below.

"Here I go!" Dandy said, doing the same. "But remember, Malcolm. There won't be any school buses on the other side when we need to get out."

Malcolm was already scouting the lot for Bus 445. "We'll worry about that when the time comes."

He unzipped his pack and removed the specter detector. "Let's rock and roll."

They wormed in and out of the bus lot, checking the numbers on each bus.

"So where's the Squealmobile?" Dandy asked.

Malcolm turned a corner. "Maybe they're working on it again. Let's check over here."

They snuck over to the bus garage, a large metal structure standing square in the middle of the lot. There it was, Old 445. Malcolm nudged Dandy. "Let's go."

Malcolm checked left then right before stepping in. Dandy followed, nervously cracking his knuckles. "It feels funny being the only ones on a school bus."

"We're not the only ones." Malcolm powered up the specter detector and flipped it on.

Yip! Yip!

"Spooky!" Malcolm griped. "You followed us?"

Dandy reached down to pet him, his hand brushing right through the phantom pooch.

"Get that yappy dog off my bus!" a voice yelled.

Malcolm and Dandy both jumped back. In the driver's seat sat a lumpy, bald ghost with a dimple on his chin the size of a belly button.

"Didn't you hear me?" the pudgy ghost barked.

"GET. THAT. YAPPY. DOG. OFF. MY. BUS!"

An Enormous Grape

Malcolm froze.

Dandy continued popping his knuckles. "Who would've guessed that our bus driver was Jabba the Hut?" he said.

The ghost wobbled in his seat. "Don't insult me. And cut out that knuckle-popping! It's annoying."

Malcolm dared to take a step closer. "Not as annoying as listening to that horn honking over and over." He reached into

his pack for the ghost zapper—the second-handiest gadget he owned.

"I've got a better idea," Malcolm said. "I'll get you off the bus."

The ghost sneered, his fat belly jiggling. "I'm not going anywhere."

"Oh yeah? Say bye," Malcolm spat, aiming the zapper at the ghost. But before he could press the trigger . . .

Hoooooooonk!

The blaring horn startled Malcolm, causing him to drop the zapper. It skittered across the floor, and rolled under a seat.

It also spooked Spooky. *Yip! Yip!* he barked as he dashed under, too.

"Uh, Malcolm?" Dandy said, inching toward the door. "Let's not bother the b-big bad gentleman haunting this bus. Maybe we should just g-go."

"You're not going anywhere!" the ghost bellowed. The bus door slammed shut, trapping them inside.

Malcolm raised his hands like he was surrendering. He could see the zapper reflected in the bus's rearview mirror. He just had to find a way to retrieve it.

But first he had to hold off the phantom driver. "Who are you?"

The ghost pointed a sausage-size finger in Malcolm's face. "None of your business."

"You're right," Dandy said. "Just let us go and we won't bother you again. Right, Malcolm? We'll just let this nice man keep honking his horn."

"Right," Malcolm said in a sly fashion. "Just let me get my dog and we'll get off your bus."

The ghost peered under the seat, then grinned back at Malcolm. "Is it your dog you want, or that zapper lying next to him?"

Malcolm leaned in, trying to look brave. "What I really want is to know who you are."

"I said it's none of your business," the ghost repeated.

"It is my business," Malcolm argued. "I have to ride this bus. I should at least know who the driver is."

"Yeah," Dandy agreed. "We have a right to know."

"You have a right to get off my bus!" The ghost inhaled a deep breath, then exhaled straight at Dandy. Dandy went flying off his feet and *wham!* came straight down on his bottom.

"Ouch!"

"Okay, okay," Malcolm said, still peeking in the mirror at the zapper. He needed to stall for time. "At least tell us your name."

The ghost shifted in his seat, his belly jiggling under his plaid shirt. "If you just

have to know, smarty, my name is George Grape. I've been the driver of this bus for ten years."

"Ten years?" Malcolm said, moving slowly toward the seat that hid the zapper. The bus was eerily quiet . . . except for Dandy cracking his knuckles.

"Yes," George answered. "And I'll stay right here until I get where I'm going."

Malcolm should have figured. It seems every ghost had a mission. He slid his foot a little closer to the seat. "Where are you going?"

The ghost heaved his fat bottom from the seat. "Why should I tell you?"

Malcolm nodded toward Dandy. "'Cause maybe we can help."

"Oh," George chuckled, "so you and Knuckles here are going to help me out?"

"We've helped lots of ghosts before."

George nudged his fat belly closer. "Yeah, helped them evaporate!"

Malcolm couldn't argue with that. He'd zapped as many ghosts as he'd helped. "Just tell us why you stay on this bus. You must have a reason."

"I have a reason all right," George said. "I've been waiting for Sheldon McFee to board."

"Who's Sheldon McFee?" Dandy asked, pulling himself up off the floor.

"Wouldn't you like to know!" George bellowed.

Malcolm took a couple of steps back, closer to the zapper. "Actually, we would."

George clenched his fists, his fingers wrapping back straight through his palms.

"Let's just say, when I find that little pip-squeak I'm going to pummel him."

Malcolm wasn't sure how old George had been when he died, but it was the first time he'd ever heard someone use the word *pummel*.

"Listen," Malcolm said, inching back. He was so close now he could hear Spooky panting, "maybe we could find Sheldon for you."

"Fine!" George bellowed. "You bring him to me." He glared at Malcolm then Dandy. "And after I finish off Sheldon, I'm going to feast on you boys."

George whipped around to Dandy. "Would you stop that?"

Malcolm saw his chance. He dove under the seat, snatched up the zapper and . . . George had disappeared.

A Bulldog with a Driver's License

It was a bumpy ride to school and back. There was the deafening horn, stuck doors, and an occasional phantom kick or pinch.

"We've got to get George off this bus," Malcolm said as thcy ncared his house.

Dandy sat hunched over with his hands covering his head. "Yeah. He's tickled me twice, bent my thumb backward, and

given me a scalp-burning noogie. He's like an invisible ninja."

The second they reached Malcolm's lab, he pulled out his computer to do a search. "Maybe there's something about him online." He typed in *George Grape*.

Dandy looked over Malcolm's shoulder. "Wow, there sure are a lot of them on the Internet. Check out this guy! They call him George Grape because he can cram seventy-five grapes in his mouth at once."

"Fascinating," Malcolm mumbled, still scanning the links.

"Do you think our George Grape did any of those things?" Dandy asked. "How are we going to know which one is him?"

"We'll just have to narrow the search." Malcolm added the words *bus driver* to the name. He got a hit. "Look. We've found him. Here's a newspaper article."

WAXBERRY SCHOOL DISTRICT NEWS

George Grape, a bus driver for the Waxberry School District, suffered a heart attack yesterday after returning from his appointed route. Officials suspect that the heart attack was brought on by a speckled kingsnake that was found curled around the gearshift. There is no indication of how the snake made it on as a passenger of the bus since snakes don't normally attend school unless brought in a mayonnaise jar for show-and-tell. Kingsnakes are not poisonous, which leads investigators to believe that the snake simply scared Mr. Grape to death. The snake has been brought in for questioning.

Malcolm leaned back against the wall. "This explains a lot."

"Yeah," Dandy agreed. "George died of a heart attack."

"And," Malcolm added, "whoever wrote that article is a total dweeb."

Dandy nodded. "I know. King snakes won't fit in a mayonnaise jar."

The article included a photo of Mr. Grape. His black hair was slicked back over his ears, and his jowls covered his collar.

"That's him all right," Dandy said. "A bulldog with a driver's license."

Malcolm nodded, clicking the computer back to the search screen. "That's George, but who's Sheldon McFee?" He typed in the name. Only one Sheldon McFee popped up.

"That's him?" Dandy asked.

They were staring at a picture of a man wearing a gray suit and holding up a large trophy. The caption under the picture read: *Sheldon McFee, honored for his efforts in building a better community.*

Dandy gave Malcolm a puzzled look. "He seems like a nice guy."

Malcolm agreed. "And look. He doesn't live too far from here. So why does George Grape want to pummel him?"

"Maybe he doesn't want a better community?" Dandy suggested.

Malcolm looked back at the photo. "Dandy, how old do you think Sheldon McFee was ten years ago?"

Dandy shrugged. "In high school, I guess."

"Right," Malcolm said. "And riding the bus."

"Do you think Sheldon rode Bus 445?" Dandy asked.

Malcolm nodded and said, "Yep. And I think he's the reason it turned into the Squealmobile."

The Chase Is On!

Saturdays are great for catching up on sleep. Except in Malcolm's house. The noise level is equal to that of a 747 zooming over a rock concert.

"Wow," Dandy said, climbing out of his sleeping bag. "What time is it?"

Malcolm looked at his watch. "Time to drive George out of the Squealmobile."

When Malcolm stepped into the hall, Grandma Eunice bounced into him with her wheelchair.

"Out of the way, Malcolm! I almost had him." She circled her chair around and pushed toward a fuzzy black caterpillar creeping along the floor.

"Uh, Grandma, where's your scooter?" Malcolm asked.

"I'm no longer the Gray Rocket," she said, aiming toward the caterpillar. "Your mom took it away. Said I was destroying the house. Can you believe that?"

Malcolm looked at Dandy. Dandy looked at Malcolm. Then they looked at the scraped paint on the walls, jagged holes in the plaster, and black skid marks on the floor. They both said, "Yeah."

"So what happens to the scooter?" Malcolm asked. "Are you going to return it?"

Grandma Eunice said, "Can't. It was a closeout."

"Oh, that's right," Malcolm said, eyeing the fuzzy creature that Grandma was determined to get. "Grandma, I don't know what you have against that caterpillar, but why don't you let us take it outside."

"But if you take it out then we can't use it," she argued.

Malcolm asked, "Use it for what?"

"I'm giving it to Cocoa for a substitute eyebrow. This worm and a little superglue will do the trick."

Malcolm scooped the caterpillar up with the bottom of his shirt and handed it to grandma. He looked at Dandy and they moved to the front door.

Heading back to the bus barn was priority one. "Think there'll be people there on Saturday?" Dandy asked as they whizzed through the shortcuts again.

"Not unless there's a field trip," Malcolm replied.

Luckily, all the buses were in place, and no one was around. No one except George Grape.

Malcolm gripped the zapper tightly. Nothing was going to startle it out of his hand this time. "Ready?" he asked Dandy.

Dandy gulped a few times, then squeaked, "Sure."

Malcolm powered up the specter detector and handed it over. "You hang on to this."

Dandy held on tight as they stepped onto the bus. There sat George behind the wheel. His pale face turned a deep shade of pink.

"Don't even think of pointing that zapper at me!" George said. The force of

his voice caused the windshield wipers to come on, the red stoplights to blink, and the nerve-racking horn to blare!

Dandy covered his ears. "Get 'im, Malcolm!"

But Malcolm was just too curious. He lowered the zapper. "Why are you after Sheldon McFee?"

George sat back, causing all the blaring, wiping, and flashing to cease. "This doesn't concern you, boy."

"As long as I'm riding this bus every day, it concerns me. I want to know," Malcolm egged.

George sneered. "Sheldon is a sniveling little bully. He sasses the teachers, hurts kids, and he pulls terrible pranks. Like putting a snake in a bus driver's glove box. He hasn't been riding the bus for a while

now. But I'm going to find him. He'll pay for that cruel practical joke."

Dandy cracked another knuckle. "Uh, Mr. Grape, I don't think Sheldon will be riding this bus anymore."

"What's Knuckles talking about?" George asked Malcolm.

"He's trying to tell you that Sheldon isn't in school anymore."

George pounded his fists against his chubby knees. "Do you know where he is?"

"Well, yeah," Malcolm answered. "But what we're trying to say is—"

"Tell me where!" George bellowed. His roar sent Malcolm and the zapper flying out of the bus and onto the pavement. Dandy was still on board.

"Help, Malcolm!" Dandy yelled.

That's when the engine kicked on and the bus shot out of its parking place at tremendous speed.

Malcolm bolted for his bike and hopped on. "I'm coming, Dandy!" He pedaled around the corner and right behind the Squealmobile.

The bus cut a sharp turn, tossing Dandy to the left. Malcolm figured that Dandy must have surrendered and told George the address. After a few more turns, the runaway bus turned onto Sheldon's street and came to a sudden halt in a ditch by his house.

For the first time in ten years, George Grape stepped off of Bus 445. "Where is he? Where's that rowdy little pest?" George continued. "He'll pay for putting a snake in my glove box!"

Malcolm led George to the fence and pointed to Sheldon. "He's right there."

Between the noise of the lawn mower and the music coming through Sheldon's earbuds, he never knew they were there. He mowed nice straight lines while singing "Yellow Submarine."

"That's not him," George complained.

"That is him," Dandy said.

George shook his head and frowned. "Can't be. Sheldon's only fifteen years old."

Malcolm hated being the bearer of bad news, but George needed to know the truth. He confessed, "George, you've been haunting that bus for ten years. Sheldon grew up. He's a nice guy now. He even won a trophy for being nice."

"But he's an evil little twerp," George said.

Malcolm stepped forward. "Not anymore. I bet he felt awful about what he did to you. He's not pulling pranks anymore."

George slumped. "Darn it. I can't hurt this guy."

"Just give it up, George," Malcolm said. "Move on."

George pointed to the ghost zapper. "Guess you're going to use that on me now, right?"

"Not if you promise to stay off our bus," Dandy said.

George sighed. "But where will I go? That's been my bus for a long time. I can't just walk away. I need to ride something."

"I have just the thing," Malcolm said. "Come with me." He led them to the corner by Malcolm's house.

"This is perfect," George said, hopping on Grandma Eunice's scooter. "Does it go fast?"

Malcolm pointed to the decals. "Does a bee like honey?"

Malcolm and Dandy waved good-bye as George tootled off down the street.

Honk!

TOOLS OF THE TRADE: FIVE USES FOR THE GHOST ZAPPER

From Ghost Detectors Malcolm and Dandy

A ghost zapper is a useful tool for a ghost detector. Here are five things you can do with your ghost zapper:

1. Use it as a paperweight to hold down homework.

2. Roll it on the floor as a toy for your ghost dog. Just be careful not to spray him!

3. Aim it at a ghost to keep it from coming at you in a fury.

4. Zap a ghost that is hurting people or animals in order to make the community a safer place.

5. Give your best friend something to do while you talk some sense into a ghost that is causing trouble.